20

Dancing dinosaur
Jurassic Attack's amazing leaps, donuts, and wheelies get the crowd roaring their approval.

21

Stomp!
The dinosaur slams down on a row of cars, flattening them.

23

Happy landing
Jurassic Attack's shock absorbers take the strain as it clears a line of cars in style.

Jurassic Attack
Make: 2002 Ford F150 custom 3D Triceratops!
Engine: 540 SVO Ford
Driver: Linsey Weenk

26

2

High profile
Power Forward is one of the most popular trucks on the circuit.

Family ties
Bounty Hunter shares the same builder as Scarlet Bandit, and the drivers of the two trucks are husband and wife.

Bounty Hunter
Like the mean Western character painted on his side, Bounty Hunter won't stop until he's got his prize!

Bounty Hunter
Make: 2002 Dodge Dakota
Engine: Chevrolet
Driver: Jimmy Creten

Flying high
Bounty Hunter can hit jumps at 60 miles an hour!

Red hot!
Scarlet Bandit's scorching leaps are guaranteed to get the fans on the edge of their seats.

Scarlet Bandit
Make: Ford Expedition
Engine: Chevrolet
Driver: Dawn Creten

Scarlet Bandit takes no prisoners!

Scarlet Bandit
This outlaw truck is fast as well as fiery.

Hunt 'em down!
Other trucks may run, but Bounty Hunter always catches up with them in the end!

ANY LAST REQUESTS?

GRAVE DIGGER

Digging it
Grave Digger's top-speed leap draws a gasp from the crowd.

Green fire
Flickering green flames decorate the front of the truck.

Reckless!
Grave Digger's go-for-it style means it takes a lot of tumbles.

Grave Digger®
Make: 1950 Chevy
Engine: 540 CI Chevrolet Bow Tie
Driver: Dennis Anderson

25

Hit the Gas!

Monster trucks have taken America by storm! These mammoth machines weigh more than 10,000 pounds, can jump more than 100 feet, and can leap over 13 cars in one go! No wonder the fans go wild! Come and meet some of the stars of the circuit.

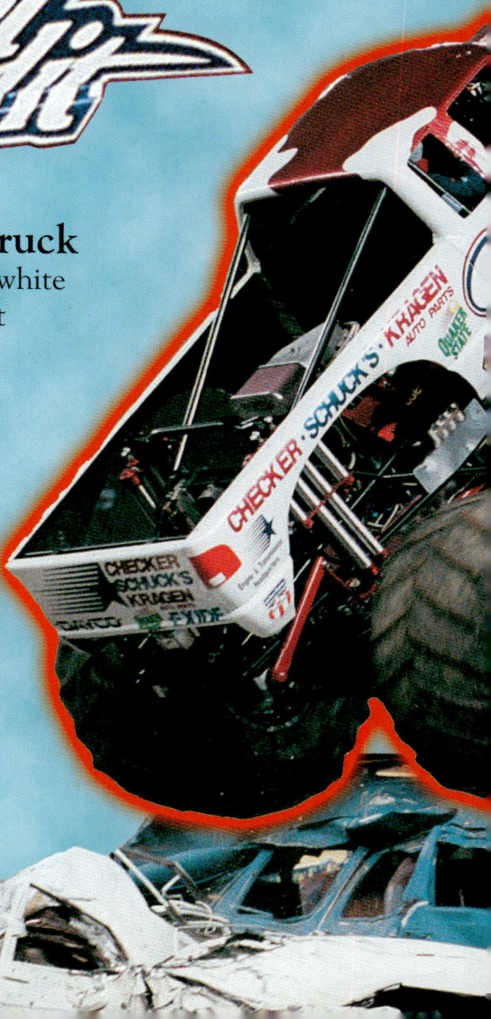

Designer truck
Striking red and white graphics cover Scarlet Bandit's bodywork.

10

Warning!
Red means danger when the scarlet raider is out on the track!

1

Scarlet Bandit

2

3

GRAVE DIGGER®

4

5

BAD TO THE BONE

6

7

POWER Forward™

8

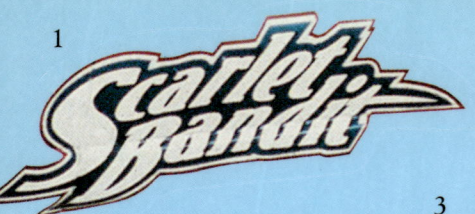

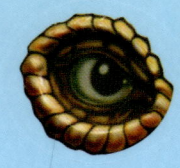

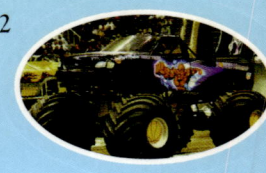

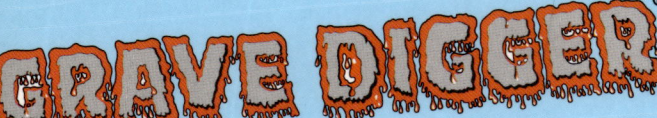

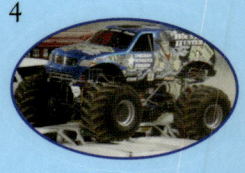

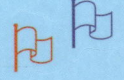

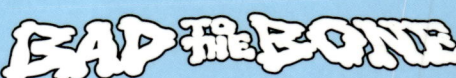

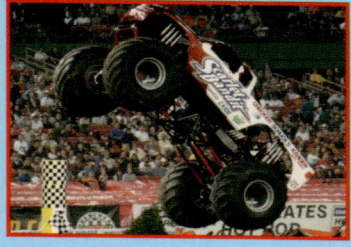

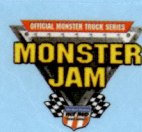

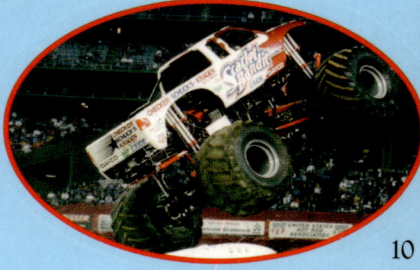

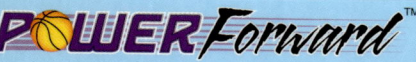

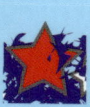

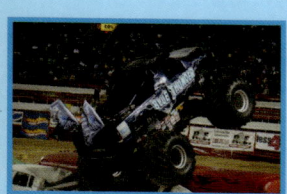

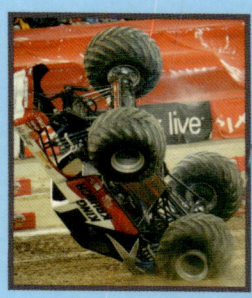

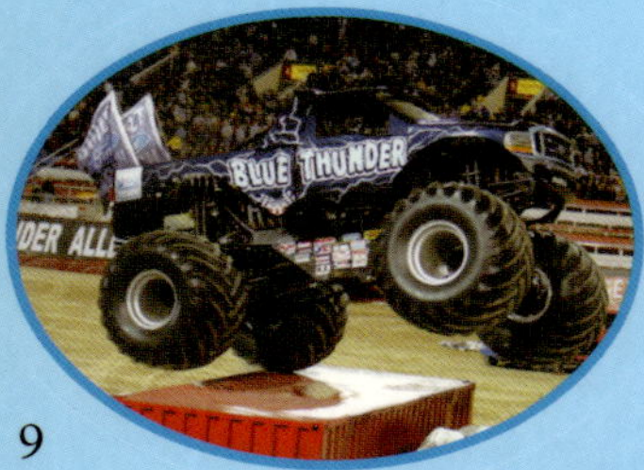

OFFICIAL MONSTER TRUCK SERIES
MONSTER JAM

10

9

12

13

11

BLUE THUNDER™

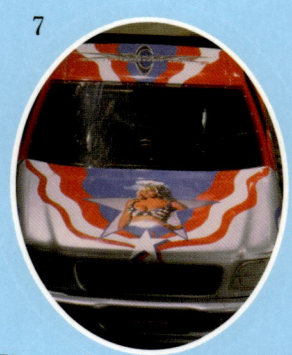

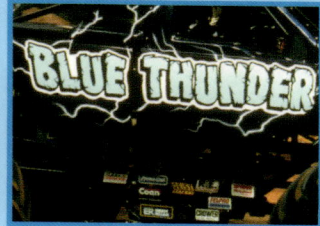

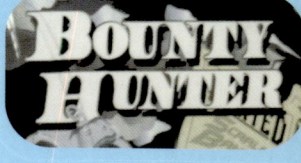

14

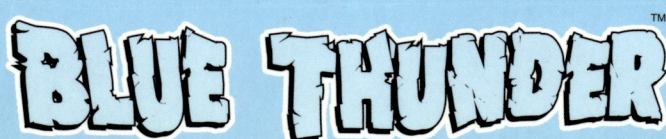

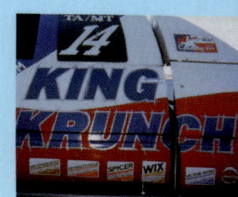

History

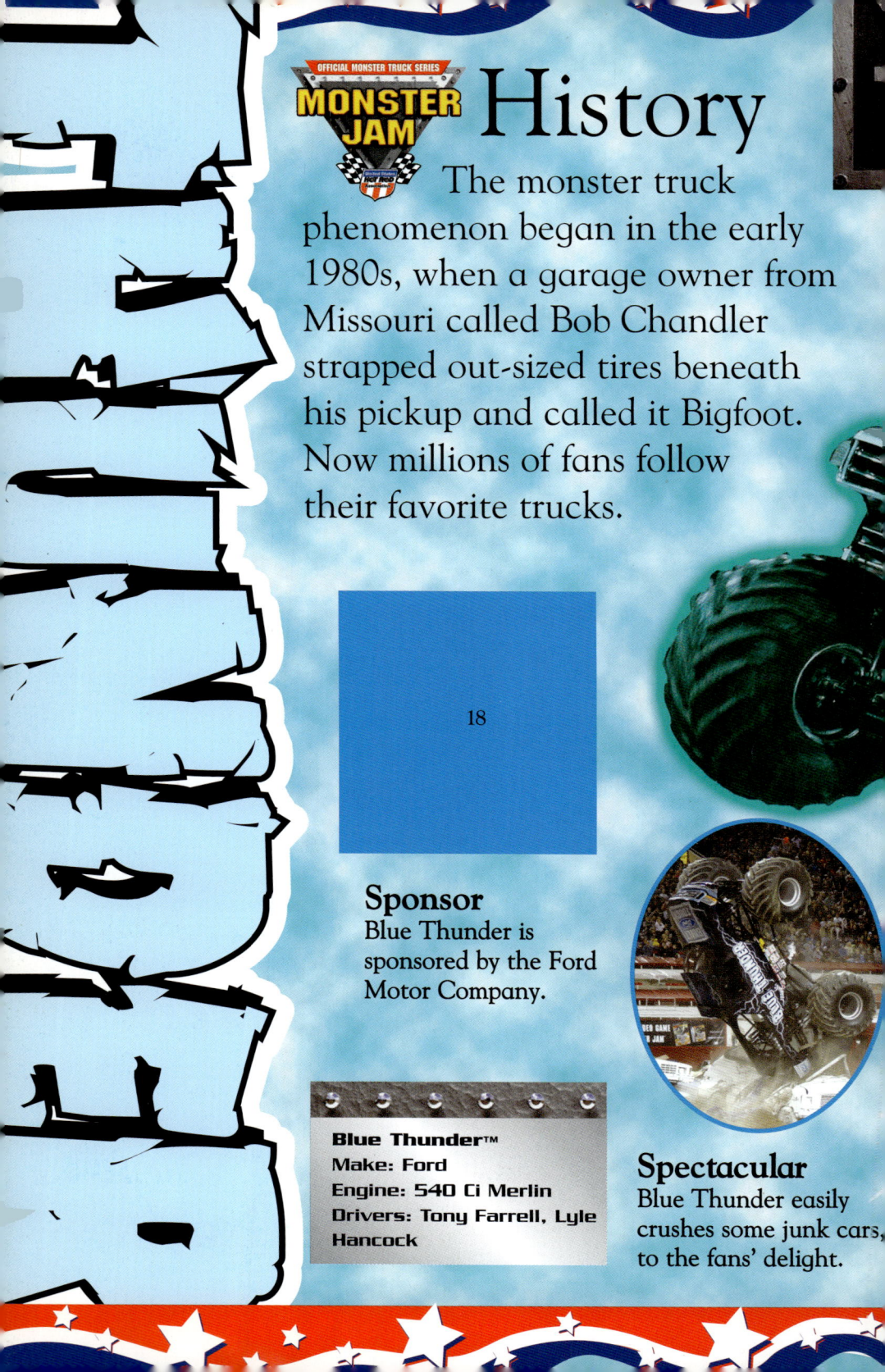

The monster truck phenomenon began in the early 1980s, when a garage owner from Missouri called Bob Chandler strapped out-sized tires beneath his pickup and called it Bigfoot. Now millions of fans follow their favorite trucks.

Sponsor
Blue Thunder is sponsored by the Ford Motor Company.

Blue Thunder™
Make: Ford
Engine: 540 Ci Merlin
Drivers: Tony Farrell, Lyle Hancock

Spectacular
Blue Thunder easily crushes some junk cars, to the fans' delight.

Let it soar!
Monster trucks can jump up to 25 feet in the air.

Blue Thunder
The hot shoes who share the driving of this prolific truck have been friends for years.

Striking!
Lightning bolts decorate the truck's name, painted on its side.

Storming!
Blue Thunder defies gravity as he leaps some junk cars.

Travelers
King Krunch and the other trucks travel to events all over the U.S.A., treating fans to displays of driving skill.

Freestyle
Madusa was trained by trucking legend Dennis Andersen. She's especially strong at freestyle events, but her racing skills are impressive, too!

King Krunch
Make: Chevrolet
Engine: 540
Driver: David Smith

Lady driver
Madusa has a portrait of her driver, wearing the stars and stripes, on the front.

Making Trucks

Monster trucks all look different, but their main ingredients are the same: a gigantic eight-cylinder engine, a steel frame, a fiberglass body, and four huge tires. A truck can take over a year to build and cost more than $150,000.

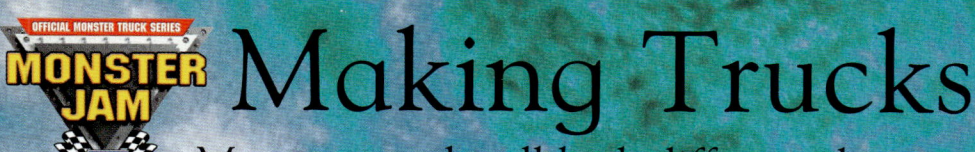

Scaled up
Jurassic Attack fixes its enemies with a scaly stare.

Jurassic Attack
This monster truck is made to look like a Triceratops dinosaur, complete with three fearsome horns!

King Krunch

Lone star
A single star shines on the truck's bodywork.

King Krunch
King Krunch is proud to hail from Texas, and the truck's design reflects the themes of the Texan state flag.

Rolling
The trucks are designed to take a pounding—and they often do!